# Broken Vessel

Tracy Henderson

Published by Tracy Henderson, 2024.

This is a work of fiction. Similarities to real people, places, or events are entirely coincidental.

BROKEN VESSEL

**First edition. June 13, 2024.**

Copyright © 2024 Tracy Henderson.

ISBN: 979-8224984992

Written by Tracy Henderson.

# Table of Contents

I would like to dedicate this book to the potter and his fine work. Although I did not get to meet him, his work left a lasting impresson on me. I also want to take the time to dedicate this book to you the reader. Couldn't do it without you

# INTRODUCTION

While attending school at Southern Illinois University in Carbondale Illinois, I was sitting in the Student Center. Across the hall from where I was sitting there was a potter. My attention was drawn to him, so I decided to move to where I could see better. I watched as the potter put the clay on the wheel. He began moving his feet on the pedals. As his feet moved, the wheel began to turn. Around and around the clay went. As the clay was spinning, the potter was molding the clay into something.

Suddenly, he saw a flaw. I watched him stop the wheel, crush the clay and start over. I stood there in amazement as the clay began to take shape. Such is the case for a nineteen year old college freshman point guard on the college football team in Whereabouts Texas.

On the outside it appeared his life was altogether. He had a charming girlfriend, a great start to a football career, and was getting his degree in Law. Behind the scenes there were cracks. His life was a mess. What you saw at school is not what you got in reality. He was a broken vessel. Would he ever get it together? We will have to follow him and watch the potter shape his life to see what becomes of this vessel.

# CHAPTER 1

He was not suppose to be alive. That is what the doctor from Whereabouts Memorial Hospital in Whereabouts Texas told his mother and father after she delivered him. He was diagnosed with a hole in his heart while he was in his mother' s womb. The doctor gave him a 50/10 chance to live. On this day, his birthday he beat the odds.

The hospital called in a heart doctor to examine the baby. When the examination was complete, the heart doctor told the parents his heart was fine. There was no hole, however, the right chamber was slightly bigger than the left chamber, and they would have to monitor him close.

That news made the parents believe in a higher power. Before the baby was born, the father said he was an atheist. "If there is a God, our baby will be fine," the father proclaimed. On this day, the father was shown there was a God. They named the child Gabriel because the said he had an angel watching over him.

Gabriel weighed six pounds five ounces. He had the cutest chubby cheeks the parents ever saw. He had a head full of brown curly hair. He had the biggest hands and feet the parents ever saw. "He is going to be tall," the mother said. When he cried, he had a set of lungs on him that demanded respect and attention. He was the perfect specimen of a healthy baby boy. He was the vessel on the wheel.

As time passed on and he started school they noticed he had a slight learning disability. He was sharp and smart, but had trouble learning things as quick as the other students did. This caused him to be made fun of when he arrived in the third grade. While the other students were ahead in their subjects, Gabriel was a grade behind them. This caused him to be picked on and not have many friends. One Sunday his mother decided to attend church with her close friend. Her friend was what she called a church nut. She believed in the power of prayer. When Gabriel's mother inquired why she was so crazy about church, her friend told her a story that changed the course of Gabriel's life forever.

This woman was diagnosed with cancer when she was twenty-one. She was given six months to live, when she was invited to a Benny Hinn crusade. Although reluctant to go, she went and was called out and prayed for. When she went back to the doctor for her next appointment, she showed no signs of cancer. She has been cancer free for over ten years now.

At church Gabriel's mother knelt at the altar and for the first time in her life, she tried to pray. "Oh God, my friend told me what you did for her. I have no reason to ask you anything for myself after the life I've lived. I'm asking you to help my son. If you help him and heal him, I will dedicate him to you for the rest of his time he lives in my house. Amen," she prayed. She did not feel any different when she got up. She thought the prayer didn't work. That night she will have an experience that will change her mind.

That night while lying in bed she felt like there was a presence standing beside her. She was always afraid of the dark ever since she was a toddler, so she was afraid to look to see what was beside her. Finally, she mustered enough courage to look. When she looked up, what she saw changed her life.

In front of her was a man standing about six- foot tall. This man had a glow that appeared to light up the whole room. She decided to turn her head and look at her husband. As she looked at him, she noticed the room was not lit up on his side. Suddenly, she turned back to see if the figure was still there. He was still standing in the same place he was.

He had a white robe on that went to the floor. On his left side was a golden sash. On his head he wore a king's crown. It was a beautiful crown. It was a big gold band with a purple top. "Daughter, I heard your prayer this morning," the man said. "Who are you?" she asked the man. "I am Jesus, and I come to personally give you a message. I could have sent an angel with this message, but I wanted to come and give it to you myself. Gabriel is a work on the wheel. Like a pot being made on a potter's wheel, Gabriel is that pot. We have plans for him, so we must purify him. Rest assured I will totally heal him in time," Jesus told her as he vanished.

Weeks passed and Gabriel began having visitations. His first visitation happened when he was in third grade. It was the Friday before Christmas and he was getting ready to go on Christmas break. He was being picked on heavily that day. One of his classmates, the class bully, pushed him, causing him to fall and get hurt. Other kids in the class were calling him names, pulling his hair, and treating him horribly. Through all of that, although he cried, he never tried to retaliate.

That night, while lying in bed something happened. He was trying to fall asleep like any other night, but on this night he was broken. As hard as he tried, he could not fight the tears that streamed down his little face. As he cried, he heard someone call his name. "Gabriel," the voice called. Gabriel tried to figure out who called his name when it happened again. "Gabriel" the voice called. This startled Gabriel. "Who are you? What do you want?," Gabriel asked.

"I am Jesus, and I have so much to share with you," Jesus said. "You're a special boy Gabriel, with a special purpose," Jesus said as he vanished. Somehow, Gabriel went right to sleep. Gabriel's sleep was peaceful that night. It was as if he was being held by angels as he slept. Although he could not see anyone, he sensed they were there, and this gave him some comfort.

The following Saturday appeared to be a normal day for Gabriel. He played for hours with his friends. They rode their bikes, played football, (which even at a young age, Gabriel excelled in football.), and they played John Madden Football 2K3. After playing with his friends, his mother took him to Dairy queen for ice cream. His favorite ice cream was peanut buster parfait.

That night, as with the other nights while asleep, he had another dream. This dream was unlike all the other dreams. Jesus was not in this dream. His grandfather was in it His grandfather died when Gabriel was three years old, so all he had was pictures of him. His grandfather stood fearless in a field of clovers.

His grandfather's favorite past time while he was alive was gardening. In this dream, he was tending the field of clovers. The colors in the field popped with radiance. The grass was a green Gabriel had never witnessed before. The grass looked like velvet. The clover had a silk look to them. His grandfather died from cancer. In this dream, his grandfather looked much younger, but he still recognized him. They began to talk about Heaven. Gabriel's mother told him that is all his grandfather had on his mind.

He shared with Gabriel about the splendors of Heaven. He shared about the river of life, the streets of gold, the walls of jasper, and the gates of pearl. "You will get a grand tour when Jesus is ready to take you Gabriel, but for now, Jesus wanted me to just tell you about these things," grandfather said.

"You are a special boy," grandfather said. Even in the dream, Gabriel began to question what made him so special. Gabriel thought of himself anything but special. "Gabriel, you are so special even the angels know you by name. Heavenly Father mentions you to Jesus many times a day. The apostles know you as well Gabriel. Don't ever let anyone on earth tell you your worth grandson. You are very valuable in Heaven, and there are going to be times Jesus is going to stretch you in order to put you on parade. It's all apart of the process," grandfather said.

As they talked the Apostle Paul walked up to them. "You must be Gabriel," Paul said. "Yes sir, I'm Gabriel,"Gabriel replied. "Don't call me sir son, I'm the least of the Apostles," Paul said. "I persecuted Christians before I came in contact with the bright light. As I was riding to do the devil's bidding, a bright light blinded me, and knocked me to the ground. Out of the light came a voice. Saul, Saul, why are you persecuting me? I didn't even know who was talking to me, until he told me he was Jesus. From that moment on, my life was never the same. You Gabriel, are going to be the Paul of your day," Paul said. All Gabriel could do was stand there in amazement. "Fight the good fight, and keep the faith son. If you do, there is a crown of righteousness waiting for you in Heaven," Paul said with excitement as he disappeared.

Gabriel could not believe what he was seeing. He was so busy listening to his grandfather and Apostle Paul that Gabriel did not realize they were no longer standing in the field of clover. They were standing on the outside of a potter's house. "Jesus wanted me to tell you that your life is a life on the wheel," grandfather said. "What does that mean?" Gabriel asked. "There are going to be many trying times in your life. It is in those times Jesus has you on the potter's wheel. He wants to bring out your best qualities, and to do so, you must be spun, broke, and spun again," grandfather said. They stood outside the potter's house for a moment observing the potter at work. Gabriel was amazed at what he was witnessing. Before he knew it, he was back in his bed fast asleep. No one was going to believe what he witnessed tonight, so Gabriel decided to keep it to himself, and ponder it in his heart. Little did he know, years later, the world would see the work on the wheel.

# CHAPTER 2

Gabriel did not have another encounter with Heaven until he was beginning his freshman year in high school. He had a great Summer vacation. His family went to Colorado on vacation. They went to the Rocky Mountains and had a great time. He didn't appear to have a care in the world while they were on vacation.

He spent quality time with his friends when they were not on vacation. Gabriel even met a girl that moved into the neighborhood right before school started. Her name was Michelle Redmond. She was a very beautiful girl. She stood about five feet seven, had blonde hair that flowed all the way down to her waist. Her father was an Apostolic preacher, and she persuaded Gabriel to go to church with her one night. This is where Gabriel's life would take a turn.

He will never forget that night he went to church with Michelle. Michelle's father preached a message entitled the Invitation. He read the scripture, *Come unto me all ye that are labored and heavy laden, and I will give you rest. Take my yoke upon you and learn of me; for my yoke is easy, and my burden is light.* He preached to fifty people as if there was hundreds. Gabriel could not get his attention off the message. It was as if he was the center of God's attention.

Her father said," You may be here under the sound of my voice, and God has chosen you for a very special task. He is extending the invitation to you to come and give him your all. He loves you so much he died. If you were the only person on earth back in his day, Jesus would have still died for you." Before he knew it, Gabriel was at the altar crying out to God. He was saved that night and baptized in Jesus name. As he came out of the water, glory was all over him. He received the gift of the Holy Ghost, and five other young people were saved, baptized and filled that night. Gabriel's life was about to change in ways he never dreamed of.

A week later during a revival his mother came and gave herself to God. That night Gabriel had another dream. In this dream he was standing in front of the Apostle Peter. Peter began to share with Gabriel about walking with Jesus. He shared with him how he saw Jesus turn the water into wine. He saw the blinded eyes opened, the deaf hear, the lame walk and the dumb talk. "You must tread carefully Gabriel. Although I walked with the Master, and saw all those mighty miracles, I didn't really know him. When it came time for me to stand up for him, I denied him three times. When I repented, I was used tremendously by Jesus. I had such a love for him that I wrote *that I may know him and the power of his resurrection; and partake of the fellowship of his suffering.* "When you truly know him you will suffer for and with him. Treasure the path you must take to get to know him. Don't be a Judas and sell him out. God is going to use you in ways you never dream, but you must be broken and remade. If you will trust the process knowing him will be your sweetest adventure. Go with God Gabriel because he is with you," Peter said. Gabriel woke up from that dream with a tear soaked pillow.

He knelt beside his bed and began to pray. As he prayed, he could feel an angelic presence. It was as if he could hear the angels singing behind him. "Thou art worthy. Thou art worthy. Thou art worthy oh Lord," he could hear them sing.

Instantly he was standing at Golgotha's hill. God showed him the scene that took place there. He watched as a weary Jesus was led up the hill. He saw a Jesus he never knew existed. This Jesus was beaten beyond recognition. His clothes were tattered and torn. He was bleeding from head to tow. On his head was a crown full of thorns. Gabriel watched as they laid him on the ground. He could hear the soldiers nail his hands into the cross. It was as if he could feel every bit of pain Jesus was feeling. He saw them pick him up and thrust the part of the cross his hands were nailed on into place with the rest of the cross. As the cross was in place, he watched them nail his feet in place on the cross.

He could hear the laughter from the soldiers. He cried as they spit upon Jesus and mocked him. Suddenly, a scene appeared behind Jesus. The scene was Gabriel standing behind Jesus in dirty clothes. As he watched, he noticed all the filth from himself was going onto Jesus. "It is finished," he heard Jesus cry. As he cried, Gabriel noticed the scene behind him changed. He no longer had dirty clothes on. His clothes were clean. "I did this all for you Gabriel. I have a plan for you," Jesus said as Gabriel was back beside his bed praying in tongues.

Gabriel's freshman year was off to a good start. He was doing what he loved to do, playing freshman football. He was a point guard, and really good at it. His team was off to a good season. They were 15 and 0 going into the playoffs. On the final game before the playoffs, the breaking of the vessel began.

Gabriel was getting ready to score the winning run when he was tackled in such a way it caused him to break his right foot. As he lay on the ground, the other team scored the win. There in front of God, the school, and his whole team Gabriel lay broken. He was rushed off the field, and sent to the hospital. At the hospital, Gabriel underwent surgery to repair his foot. He broke his foot while the team was out of the playoffs.

While in the hospital recovering he had a dream. He saw Jesus sitting at a potter's wheel working on a vessel. The vessel appeared to have it altogether, when suddenly, Jesus stopped working. He watched Jesus crush the vessel, working it back into a lump of clay. Jesus looked at Gabriel with piercing eyes of love as he restarted the work on the wheel. At that moment Gabriel woke up from the dream, as he had a room full of company.

Some of the players decided to come see him. They were accompanied by Melissa, who faithfully stayed by Gabriel's side through his ordeal. They cheered Gabriel up, letting him know he did not let the team down in the playoffs. For some reason, some called it a miracle, the referees reviewed the play and noticed Gabriel was fouled when he broke his foot. The decision was reversed, and his team was in the playoffs. Gabriel would be on the sidelines cheering his team on. His replacement was not as good as he was. The whole team knew this, but it was as if God made him stand out from all the rest of the players. "God why is this happening to me?" Gabriel asked when he was told the news. "I'm doing this to keep you humble before me Gabriel. Trust the process," God replied. No one, not even Melissa heard the answer God gave, but she knew from the smile that was on

Gabriel's face he got his answer. "It well be well. We will win the playoffs," Gabriel told the team.

The following week was the playoffs. Gabriel fasted that whole day asking God to help his replacement to shine. "God, Joe must increase for the playoffs while I decrease until next year," Gabriel prayed. Joe played the games like he never had the whole season. He played so well, he ended up winning the most improved player award. He took his team all the way to victory in the playoffs. This would be the first time in the school's sixty year history they were crowned champions in football. The coach and the team praised Joe's ability, while humbly and thankfully, Gabriel gave praise to God.

As the freshman year progressed Gabriel had some ups and downs. He had just got out of the cast when he re- injured his foot in P.E. He was playing basketball and went up for a shot. The kid guarding him went up with him and accidentally bumped him. He landed on his foot and it was broken again. He spent another six weeks in a foot cast. The doctor said he may never be able to play football again. This news troubled him, so he went home and started praying. As he prayed, Paul appeared to him again. "War a good warfare Gabriel," Paul said.

Gabriel began questioning what he meant. "I was ship wrecked, beaten, imprisoned, but I kept pressing on," Paul said. Gabriel wiped the tears from his eyes as he intently listened. "God would not bring you to this mountain if he wasn't going to help you get through it," Paul added as he disappeared. Suddenly the woman with the issue of blood appeared to Gabriel. She didn't say a word to him, but her actions told the story.

He saw the way she pressed her way in through the crowd. He saw someone jump ahead of her, and she went around them. This happened many times on her journey to Jesus. As she walked she left a trail of blood behind her. She looked faint, but determined. Finally, she got to her goal. As she met the master, she touched the border of his garment. How could she not touch it? Someone pressed behind her knocking her into Jesus. Gabriel watched as virtue transferred from Jesus into this woman. Suddenly, she stood upright whole. Gabriel knew although the doctor gave him this report, he must get persuaded.

Gabriel refused to let his broken foot deter him. He wanted to play football again. Once the cast was off, he took physical therapy serious. Within a matter of weeks his foot was better, and the doctor gave him a release. He was able to play football the following year as long as he did not injure himself again.

Gabriel and Melissa grew closer together. Gabriel was a faithful member of the church. Sin lies at the door for preacher's kids just like any other kid. Melissa and Gabriel was able to fight the temptation to have sex multiple times. As hard as it was they trusted God would bring them through. At the Valentines dance things would be different. The spirit was willing to help them, but their flesh was weak. They ended up having sex. After the act, they both prayed asking for forgiveness. Gabriel, hard as it was, broke the news to her parents. Instead of condemning them, his parents admonished them and prayed with them. Melissa and Gabriel grew closer together, although they didn't have sex again.

Weeks passed since Gabriel and Melissa's encounter. Gabriel loved Melissa very much. Melissa was in love with Gabriel as well. As freshmen, kids are growing up, yet are still experimenting with their new found emotions. Such was the case for Gabriel and Melissa. They were in love, and even had this sexual encounter, but something seemed to be missing. What exactly Gabriel could not put his finger on. The more he prayed the more complex the questions became.

One day, while in prayer, the answer finally came. Gabriel had a vision that troubled him. He saw Melissa walking down the aisle in a beautiful white wedding dress. The dress flowed down her body. The veil was so long she had to have someone carry the bottom of it for her. Waiting at the altar was Gabriel and Jesus. As Melissa reached Gabriel and Jesus, her father put her hand in Gabriel's. Jesus, put his hand on top of the couple's hand. "As you two are my bride, if you will truest me, she will become your bride," Jesus said as Gabriel came out of the vision.

He could not believe what he saw or heard. He was hesitant about telling Melissa, but felt compelled to tell her in front of her parents. Much to Gabriel's surprise, Melissa had the same vision. Her father, the stern Hell fire and brimstone preacher, and her meek and mild mother also had visions of that day.

With tears in his eyes, her father shared with everyone his vision. The family invited Gabriel over for dinner, as was the custom since they got together. The setting was not a modern day setting, but appeared to be back in Bible times. Jesus was serving the family when suddenly it appeared they were at the wedding banquet portrayed in the Bible. As Jesus was preparing the drink for the wedding guests, he spoke, "I have blessed this union. Gabriel is a work on the wheel of the master. Do not kick against the pricks, and fight my plan for your daughter's life. She will not only be a pastor's daughter, be a pastor's wife to the nations. I am preparing Gabriel and your daughter for the nations. Just as I turned the water into wine, I will turn their hearts toward the nations,"

No one knew Melissa wanted to go to the nations. No one knew Gabriel had a vision of him standing on the soil of Japan. Jesus knew these things though. Without hesitation, Gabriel jumped out of his chair, got down on one knee and asked Melissa to marry him in the future. With tears in her eyes, she accepted his proposal. The whole room was filled with joy and excitement. It was as if glory rested on the entire house that day.

Gabriel was afraid to tell his mom the news. She was a good mother, but there were lines she dared not to blur. When he mustered up the courage to tell her, she smiled with approval. She had a dream the night before. A messenger came to the door with an invitation. As she opened the envelope, she saw it was an invitation to her son's wedding. At the bottom of the invitation was written, marriage blessed by God.

She liked Melissa, and really hoped she was being accepting of Melissa marrying Gabriel. When she found out she was the one, Gabriel's mother rejoiced with Gabriel. As they embraced she told Gabriel the dream she had. Gabriel did not expect her to be so accepting, but when God steps in, miracles happen.

Gabriel and Melissa' s freshman year was coming to a close. Aside from his mishap of breaking his foot twice, the school year was great. This was the year he met Melissa and where his life was changed forever. On the last day of their freshman year, Gabriel realized his position on the potter's wheel.

He was in the car with his mother driving home. Suddenly a car ran a stop sign and slammed into the passenger's side of the car. Gabriel was injured in the accident. The extent of the injuries were unknown at the scene. The driver of the other car was killed. As they were investigating the scene, it was discovered the driver, an elderly man, had a fatal stroke that killed him before impact. This caused Gabriel considerable trauma.

At the hospital, after being examined, Gabriel learned he had only minor scrapes and bruises. There were no broken bones whatsoever. For weeks Gabriel had nightmares about the gentleman that hit them. As hard as Melissa tried, she could not console him enough, so she went to war for him in prayer.

As she prayed, Jesus appeared to her. "He is on the wheel Melissa. War a good warfare for him, and allow me to work in his life," Jesus said. The more she prayed and warred the more the battle raged. Satan was trying to cause Gabriel to lose his mind. Gabriel would not ride in a car for about three weeks. Every time he got near a car he trembled. Finally, on a Sunday night, God delivered him from this trauma.

He was praying for a young man at the altar when Melissa's dad went over and slayed hands on Gabriel. He began casting out the spirit of fear. As they were praying, you could hear popping sounds. It was chains of fear being broke off of Gabriel. As he got up from the altar, he hugged Melissa for the first time since the accident. He was free and back to being the Gabriel she loved.

# CHAPTER 3

The Summer of the end of Gabriel and Melissa's freshman year going into their sophomore year was very eventful for the couple. As with any Summer, it started out very dry and slowly picked up momentum. For the first few weeks of Summer, Gabriel was in football camp. He loved football camp because the coach pushed him beyond his limitations in order to bring out the best in him. Just as a potter works the clay and works the clay to get the smoothest possible framework to work with, the coach did the same for Gabriel.

Gabriel was promoted to quarterback. He was the perfect size for the position. He had the skill and the charisma of a quarterback, the coach made sure of it. There were days in the process where Gabriel did not think he could be pushed any more than he was already being pushed. It was during those times he would hear a voice in his spirit telling him, "as the potter works and molds the clay, so I am molding you. You will be a vessel of honor." Suddenly, he would get strength he never knew he had. Some would say he had supernatural strength.

One night after a vigorous football camp session, Gabriel went home and fell asleep on the couch. He was instantly escorted to the throne room. Sitting on his throne was God the father. He was a huge person. He was as tall as he was huge. Electricity protruded from the throne he was sitting on.

The grass and the trees were swaying in unison as if they were giving him praise. Behind him was the river of life. The fish were jumping up out of the water giving glory to God. Around the throne were an in-numeral host of angels. The number was beyond counting. They had a wide wingspan. They would fly up over the throne and come back down. When they got back on the ground, they folded their wings as a human would take off their hat to the Star Spangled Banner. "Holy, holy, holy, Lord God almighty. Who was and is and is to come," the angels sang. As the father was being worshiped, he would smile and glory would overshadow him.

Suddenly, all the noise stopped for a brief moment. God looked at Gabriel and said, "the potter knows the clay. He knows how much pressure the clay can take. He knows how many times he needs to spin the wheel. While the potter is doing his work, he never takes his inner eye off the finished product. You my son, are on the potter's wheel, but your design is continually before me. I know your beginning and I know your ending. When you feel you can take no more pressure, my strength will come upon you, and my glory will surround you. You can endure Gabriel. All you have to do is be the clay and let me be the potter. I have your design ever before me." Suddenly Gabriel woke up from the dream. He could feel a thickness in his room. It wasn't threatening and did not scare him. Suddenly, his inner man recognized that glory was surrounding the room, and Gabriel slept peacefully the rest of the night.

As football camp came to a close two weeks later, Gabriel and Melissa was getting ready to go on a trip with the youth group of the church. They were going on a missionary trip. Gabriel was excited he was attending the trip. He knew God had something special in store for the youth group.

The youth group went to the place where the Azuza Street revivals took place. They stood on the same ground as the saints of old did during those revivals. The building was still standing, and they were allowed to go inside. Gabriel wanted to stand in the same place William Seymour sat with a box over his head. As he stood there admiring the place, a voice spoke to him,"As I was with Pastor Seymour, I will be with you. I am giving you the same mantle he had on him when he was alive. This transfer mantle will revolutionize your life, but you will pay a heavy price to keep it," the voice said. Suddenly, Gabriel felt electricity go all through him. Melissa told him he stood in that place and lit up life a Christmas tree. She knew it was the glory of God resting upon him.

As Gabriel stood where Seymour sat, he began to witness to those in attendance. As he began to speak, the youth group could hear a sound of wind blowing through the room. One by one the wind blew upon each of the youth in attendance. They erupted in harmonious praise and worship. The sick were made whole. In attendance was a boy that was suffering from Muscular Dystrophy. As Gabriel was speaking, the boy was instantly healed. This caused the youth group to erupt in higher praise.

The trip lasted a week. The glory of God transformed the youth group of Gabriel and Melissa's church. All the youth knew Gabriel and Melissa were engaged to get married at a later date. The couple were waiting on the timing of the Lord. Suddenly, God spoke to both of them,"it is time," he said. Melissa ran out of the building and immediately called her dad for advice. Her father agreed with what they heard. Gabriel's mother also agreed with it. Gabriel and Melissa sat on the same pew William

Seymour sat and got married. It was unheard of for a sophomore couple to get married. People were surly going to talk, but they knew that had to obey God. Where would they live? What would people say? After the ceremony, the youth group left for home. They knew God met them at the same place lives were transformed all those years ago. For Gabriel and Melissa, it was more than a missionary trip. They knew what God did on Azuza Street, he was going to do with them. It would be just like it was with Elisha. They would do double the works William Seymour ever did in his entire lifetime.

As with any great moves, anytime there is a move there is also resistance. The youth group soon witnessed their battle. The youth group told the church the great things that took place during the missionary trip. The church rejoiced until they found out Gabriel and Melissa were married. Soon the rumors started flying through the church. She must be pregnant. The pastor is an unfit parent. Gabriel's mom was an unfit parent. Those kids lacked discipline. All those rumors were going through the church. Soon, the rumors reached the district headquarters.

The following Sunday morning a member for headquarters made a visit to the church. The pastor had no idea why he was there, although the congregation did. After church he interviewed the pastor. The district representative told the pastor he was being accused of misconduct by allowing his Sophomore daughter to get married. He wanted to know why this was allowed to happen.

With a holy boldness the pastor informed the representative that God told them to get married, and that he had a vision they were married on this trip. The pastor, under the unction of the Holy Ghost, began telling the representative things about his family know one else knew. He had two daughters that were pregnant out of wedlock. After he told the representative, the report was unfounded. He was asked whether he would be interested in resigning from this church and he could take over as Senior pastor in a much bigger church. To this the pastor agreed, and his family was preparing to leave the following week.

This news troubled Gabriel and Melissa. Were they going to have to move too? Were they going to be allowed to live together? What was their future going to be like? All of those questions were answered when the pastor decided to move Gabriel's family to the new area. God joined this couple and he was not going to break it up.

With a new start comes new opportunities. Gabriel and Melissa were put in charge of the Junior church. Since they moved to a new area, Gabriel's football charter was moved to a new school. While he was excited about it, he also had other feelings about it. He was going to miss his team. They were not just a team, but they were brothers.

Melissa found herself involved in cheer leading. She always wanted to be a cheer leader but was never able to make the squad. At the Jesus Name Apostolic high School she made the squad. She was so excited. She would get to cheer for her husband out on the football field. The couple would also get to play other christian schools in the area, and this excited them even more. Yes Gabriel loved going to public school, but he was beginning to feel the weight of the world trying to jump on his shoulder.

During football camp one of his former squad mates tried to get him to try vaping and some drugs. He was so afraid he was going to give in to such temptation if he stayed at the school. He was amazed when God moved him to a christian school.

As Summer progressed Gabriel got deeper into sports. He played baseball that Summer. It appeared his time was being taken away from Melissa and this was beginning to cause a rift. They loved each other unconditionally, but something had to give. He was beginning to waver in his faith because of sports. This scared him, and he and Melissa went heavily into prayer. "Drop out of sports," a voice spoke to his spirit. Gabriel began to try ad sort things out in his head trying to find ways to stay in sports. "Drop out of sports," the voice said again. Again, the thoughts were running through his mind. "Drop out of sports or blood will be upon your hands," the voice spoke in a matter of fact tone. He told Melissa what he had to do. She agreed with him, and she dropped out of cheer leading.

Gabriel was offered a spot on the college football team when he graduated high school. All he had to do was keep his grades up from his Sophomore to his Senior year. He was troubled about this because it was his dream. On one hand he wanted to do it, on the other, he did not want blood to be on his hands. He had a decision to make. Does he play football in the coming season or does he drop out and forfeit his spot on the college team? He discussed this with the football coach. The coach was in the same situation Gabriel is in when he was in school. It was as if the potter was calling the shots and giving the coach the solution. He decided to take Gabriel's resignation. Since Gabriel came highly recommended from his high school and his stats with the team were high enough, Gabriel's spot on the college team was secured for a lifetime. He was able to be on the college team whether he played football in high school again or not. Gabriel could feel his life being smoothed around the edges with this news. He could devote his time to family and still go to college and play football. Gabriel took the coach up on his offer.

As the Summer progressed so did some challenges for Gabriel. He felt as if God was trying to teach him how to practice self denial. While him and Melissa was in one of their morning prayer sessions Gabriel had a vision. In his vision he was standing on a stage. On he stage were four doors. On one door was a sign that said my ambitions. All the other doors had signs that had different choices a person faces in life. In front of Gabriel was a man. He directed Gabriel to choose a door.

Gabriel walked to each door reading what was posted on it. When he got to the door of his ambitions, sitting on the outside of the door were things he enjoyed. At the other doors people were standing outside of them. One looked hungry, one was hurting, and one was crippled. The man told him to choose which door he would choose. As he surveyed the area, suddenly his door did not look appealing to him. He began to see pitfalls and dangers that awaited him outside that door.

In the vision, Gabriel gravitated toward the doors where the greatest needs were. As he walked toward the doors he heard Jesus say,"If any man will come after me, let him deny himself; Take up his cross and follow me."Suddenly, he noticed his door burst into flames. As the flames died down something appeared that he was familiar with. It was a sign written with the flames just like they used in the homecoming football game he played in. The sign said YOUR WORKS, then disappeared.

In the middle of the stage facing the other doors was a cross. As the people standing outside the doors looked toward the cross, what they were struggling with broke off of them and hit the ground. "your works will burn up under my intense glory. If you look toward the cross and deny your ambitions, lives will be touched and you will point the lost, the dying, the crippled, and hurting to the cross. What are you going to choose Gabriel?" he heard Jesus say. As the prayer session ended, Gabriel knew giving up sports was just the beginning. There were there were other things in his life he had to give up. In order to have God's best on his life, he had to deny himself. Some things would be easy to give up while others would feel like death. Gabriel had to pay the price.

Weeks passed and it was time to register for school. Gabriel and Melissa's Summer was eventful. Some things were pleasant such as the missionary trip and getting married. Some things were hard to bear. They learned the night before they were to register for school Melissa was pregnant. While they were full of joy, Gabriel was also full of apprehension. He wanted Melissa to have this child but was he ready for the trials that would come with the pregnancy? "My grace is sufficient for you," Jesus whispered to him. This gave Gabriel a sense of peace on one hand, and dread on the other. He knew he was being stretched more than he thought he would be able to bear. He wondered if William Seymour was stretched this far. That night he had a dream. In the dream he was back in the church at Azuza Street sitting on the front row. Suddenly a figure appeared and sat down beside him. This figure was a huge African American man. He had a look that told you he came on business. The man was William Seymour. He sat down beside Gabriel and as was his custom when he was alive, he put a box over his head.

"Do you know why I put a box over my head?" William asked. "No," Gabriel replied. "To block out any outside influences that would try to sway me," William said. That seemed to make sense to Gabriel. "If you can't see what is around you then you have to truest in things you cannot physically see. This is a faith walk son," William said. It was as if a light went off in Gabriel's head. The vision of the four doors begin to make sense to him even in this present vision.

"You can get clouded by all the hype, the pomp and the circumstance and lose what is the most important in life. When I put the box over my head I don't see anything from the outside world. I'm able to see what's inside. Glory does not come from the outside, it starts from the inside and destroys the outside. Does this make sense?," William asked. "Yes it does," Gabriel replied. "The revival was birthed because one man dared to be different. One man dared to block out the outside influences. HE was willing to reach for the invisible instead of depend on the visible. To grab the intangible and leave the tangible alone. That is how the revival was birthed, and how the new will be birthed again," William said. "I'm willing to be that one person even if I have to stand alone," Gabriel said. "There will come a time when the only person you will have to stand beside you is God. When that happens son, you will see revival. Dare to be different Gabriel. Dare to be the one that is willing to put a box over your spiritual head to block out the outside influences, and watch God. See you again soon," William said as the vision ended.

The next day while in morning prayer Gabriel was again escorted to Heaven. He was in a place he had never seen before. He was standing on the bank of a river when a man walked up to him. This man was nothing to behold. He was of medium height with long silver hair and beard. His clothes were ratty and he was covered in what appeared to be slime. Gabriel knew right away from reading the Bible this was Jonah.

"Hi Gabriel, my name is Jonah. Jesus sent me to talk to you about obedience," Jonah said. If anyone learned the hard way about obedience it was Jonah. Gabriel recalled the story. Jonah was told to go to Nineveh but tried going somewhere else instead.

"Obedience," Gabriel said. "Yes Gabriel, obedience," "From what I read in the Bible that was a sore subject for you," Gabriel said. "Indeed it was," Jonah said. Jonah stood there for a moment as if he was collecting his thoughts. "God was grooming me for success. I was pliable in his hands before I disobeyed," Jonah said. "What do you mean Jonah?" Gabriel asked.

With a sad look on his face Jonah went on. "Disobedience caused delay in my life. Because I thought I knew more than God I was not going to Nineveh to preach. I spent three days in the belly of a fish. Three days Gabriel. Some compare my three days to Jesus' three days in the grave, and actually call me a type of Jesus. While that may be true in a small sense, it is untrue if you look at the big picture. Jesus was in the grave for three days fulfilling his destiny. I was in the fish's belly three days delaying mine. Disobedience causes setback. You are on the potter's wheel for a reason. Someday, and I do not know when, your obedience is going to be put to the test. Maybe it has been already. God has your Nineveh picked out. He needs your yes Gabriel. Look what happened when I finally gave him my yes. God's no's in your life now will be his greater yes in the future if you give him your yes in every area of your life," Jonah said.

"Why did you get mad when Nineveh listened to the message you brought?" Gabriel asked. Jonah stood there a moment pondering the question. With a sad countenance he answered, "Pride. I was an arrogant man before the fish. I knew God was going to destroy the city and I thought it was a waste of time when there were other cities that needed saving. You see Gabriel, my heart was not in the right place at the time. I wanted the glory instead of God getting the glory. It cost me. To give God the glory you must be obedient to him in every area of your life. Disobedience is the result of pride. Pride will kill you. Pride will delay you. I was mad because I was very prideful. Once God spoke to me and let me know who was in charge I repented, but something no one knows because it was not recorded. My life was cut short because of disobedience. I did not live much longer after Nineveh because God took me home. If he would have let me live, I may be in Hell now instead of talking to you," Jonah said.

Jonah gave Gabriel such powerful revelation. He had no idea Jonah's life was cut short. He knew Jonah was only mentioned two other times in the Bible but never knew why. Gabriel purposed in his heart right then to remain humble and obedient. Not only was his life depending on it, but his families existence was depending on it. Jonah's confession caused Gabriel to come out of his vision. With tears in his eyes Gabriel repented in case there were times he was like Jonah.

# CHAPTER 4

As Gabriel and Melissa were getting ready to start their sophomore year of high school Gabriel's mother got sick. She has always had stomach trouble, and thought it was just another episode. Her trouble started a week before Gabriel was to go back to school. Instead of getting better as it had in the past it got worse. She could hardly keep any food down. All she was able to keep down was jello and liquids. She got worried when she began throwing up blood.

When she went to see her doctor they ran all sorts of tests on her. Her diagnosis was not good. She never expected to get the kind of news the doctor's office gave her. She had stage 4 cancer. It started in her stomach and was spreading to her liver. She was stunned when the doctor told her there was nothing he could do for her, and that she had at the most six months to live.

How was she going to tell Gabriel? This would crush him. He has so much going for him, and for him to receive this news would be disaster. She held the dreadful news in as long as she could. When Gabriel asked her what the doctor said, she decided now was the time to tell him. She gave Gabriel the diagnosis the doctor gave her. The moment she said cancer, he ran out of the room they were in, and into the room he and Melissa were staying in.

As he entered the room he hit his knees and began to sob. "Oh God, how can this be happening?" Gabriel cried. "This is so unfair. What wrong has my mother done to anyone? Does she really deserve this? Gabriel asked. Suddenly Gabriel sensed he was not alone. He began to look around, and standing by his side was an ancient looking old man. He had a burlap robe on with a ragged sash. His hair was past his shoulders and white. His beard was white and hung down to his belly. "Don't be afraid," the man said. "Who are you?" Gabriel asked. "I am Abraham, and Jehovah sent me to talk to you," Abraham said.

"Son, you must let go, and be willing to let God be God," Abraham said. "She's my mother," Gabriel replied. "Lay her down," Abraham said. "Lay her down?" Gabriel asked. "Yes, lay her down," Abraham said. "How?" Gabriel asked.

"When my son Isaac was born he was my flesh and blood. It is true I had Ishmael as a son too. Ishmael was born of the world because I rushed ahead of God, and did not wait on my Isaac. When Sarah had Isaac God gave me a test. I was to take my son Isaac, the one he picked out for me, and I was to offer him as a sacrifice. It would have been easy to question God. Gabriel, I, like you, was heartbroken and devastated. I really didn't want to give him up, but I wanted God's best for my life. I took Isaac up to the place where I was to sacrifice him. All the thoughts Satan tried to put in my mind, but I remained steadfast. When we got to where we were going, I went up with Isaac and started to sacrifice him. In the thicket, out of my natural sight was a ram. Why didn't I see it before I went up the hill? I believe it appeared after I was obedient to the call. God provided the lamb and Isaac lived," Abraham said.

Gabriel looked confused at Abraham. How was this related to his mother. It was as if Abraham knew what he was thinking.

"Obedience does not make sense at times," Abraham said. At times, obedience will break your heart. At times obedience will rip your heart out, but there is always a ram in the thicket. As you obey. God provides," Abraham said. Suddenly he looked up as if hearing a voice. "Jehovah told me to tell you she shall not die but live. She may pass from this life, but she will be alive in the world to come," Abraham said. "Obey God, and the ram will be provided," Abraham continued.

Suddenly Jesus appeared and stood beside Abraham. "I am the way, the truth and the life Gabriel," Jesus said. "Your mom will live through this. She has prayed and touched the hem of my garment. I have came to heal her," Jesus said. Gabriel smiled at Jesus and went to thank him, when in Jesus' hand appeared a lump of clay. "This is you Gabriel. Allow me to continue to mold you as a potter molds this clay. I mold you through trials and tests. You will make it," Jesus said as he and Abraham disappeared.

Gabriel shared with Melissa and the rest of er family what took place. They all took turns praying around the clock for Gabriel's mother. The more they prayed the worse she seemed to be getting. The family knew they were in spiritual warfare on her behalf. On one hand they hear the angels say don't give up. On the other hand they hear Satan tell them to give up. Finally, the family prayed together at the dinner table. As they were holding hands around the table, Gabriel heard Jesus ask him "Are you going to give in or press in?" "I'm going to press in," Gabriel said out loud. Melissa looked at him wondering who he was talking to. Her father explained to her Jesus was demanding Gabriel make a decision whether to let her live or die. He chose life.

The battle for her life kept raging on. Gabriel and Melissa went to school during the day and prayed through the night for his mother's healing.

A week passed since they began warring for her life. She had another doctor's appointment to go to. Gabriel and Melissa missed school to go with her. The doctor did another examination and scan to see if there was progression. To his amazement, there was no sign of cancer. He showed them the previous scans. Gabriel saw for himself the cancer was there in that scan. As they looked at the next scan it was completely normal. The doctor could not believe what he was seeing. Gabriel knew what took place. God provided a ram for his mother.

The school year started like any other year. A lot of hustle and bustle. Making new friends, and getting used to new classes. Gabriel and Melissa were blessed. They had each other, and the day before school started, God performed a miracle in Gabriel's mom. If that was the start of the school year, what dis God have in store for the year?

Melissa had a little apprehension about starting school because since she got pregnant over the Summer, she knew she would be a mother before the end of the school year. She was happy being a wife and mother to be. The issue was she was going to fall behind in school, and did not want to repeat her sophomore year. When she shared her worry with Gabriel, he went into prayer with her immediately. As they prayed, Melissa experienced something she never had before.

She had her first vision. Standing in front of her was Mary the mother of Jesus. She had on a beautiful blue robe with a white turban on her head. The pictures she sees of Mary in real life do not do what she is seeing justice. The paintings paint her as a beautiful woman, but a tired looking woman as well. The Mary she was seeing was beyond beautiful. She was not only arrayed in beauty, but she was also arrayed in glory. She did not have the white halo over her head like the paintings show. She was surrounded by radiance from head to toe. Her smile could melt mountains. Her eyes were so penetrating they could look deep into your soul just like an x ray machine looks at your bones. There was no question you had that was hidden from her. She was, after all, the mother of Jesus.

"Do not be afraid Melissa," Mary said. "You will not miss a beat. God has your destiny in the palm of his hand," Mary said. "But I'm going to fall behind in school," Melissa told Mary. "No, daughter, you are going to excel like no other female student in your whole class. Trust the process. Just as John leaped inside the womb of Elizabeth when we came in contact with one another, the Holy Ghost will leap inside you and propel you forward. Trust the process," Mary said as she disappeared. Melissa began praying intensely in her prayer language. As she was praying, Gabriel stopped to listen. He could understand what she was saying. Suddenly, the couple could hear angels singing in the room.

"You are chosen for a time as this. You are chosen to come forth. You are chosen as vessels of clay," the angels sang. Peace swept over Melissa like she has never felt before. She was going somewhere in God and nothing was going to stand in her way.

A week after school started football season was in full swing. It saddened Gabriel because he had to give up his spot on the team. Yes, he could have been a star. Mediocre star at best. Yes, he could have scored the winning touchdowns in the game. Yes, he could have been admired by the school, and been the hero. All of that was what he longed for in school. Gabriel knew that was his Isaac. Gabriel knew he had to lay Isaac down in order to receive the best God had for him in life. When he laid his mother's problem down God healed her. Gabriel realized he had his own living, breathing Isaac, and his Isaac was kicking and screaming for attention. "Lord, I gave up football for you, but I never laid it down like Abraham did Isaac. You take my desire to play football and turn it around for your glory," Gabriel prayed to himself. "Done," he heard the Spirit say. Suddenly there was a peace come over Gabriel and he knew things would work out.

That day the students had to sign up for clubs if they wished to participate. Gabriel was not a club person. He was a football person. Clubs never interested him unless there was shoulder pads and a football attached. He was getting ready to throw the paper of the club listings away when a club caught his eye. Friends in Christ Club. "Join it," the spirit prompted Gabriel, and he joined the club. He found out Melissa joined the club too although she was not interested in clubs like he was. What was God up to?

The couple watched God do some amazing things in the club. They saw souls be won to Christ. Students and teachers as well were getting healed. One girl, a senior, was battling depression. She has been battling depression for five years. Her mother and sister were killed in a car accident leaving her, her dad, and three brothers alone. She tried several times to commit suicide, but God spared her life. On the club meeting before homecoming she experienced her own homecoming. Like the prodigal son, she was welcomed into the family of God with open arms. Not only was she born again, but she was set free of depression.

Another student, a freshman was healed and came out of his wheelchair. He was paralyzed from his neck down, and has been for years. When he was five years old he was taking swimming lessons. He was going off the dive when he hit his head on the bottom paralyzing him. On the same day the girl was healed delivered of depression, he was healed on paralysis. The spirit of God was so think in the school, you could sense him even walking the halls. Students and teachers alike that were in the halls were slain in the spirit as he walked up and down the halls of the school.

A week after homecoming Melissa went into labor. After fifteen grueling hours of labor she delivered a healthy baby boy. As the family was rejoicing Gabriel heard Jesus speak to him," here is your Isaac." This startled Gabriel. What was Jesus meaning? What was he going to have to do in order to please God? "Here is your Isaac, are you ready and willing to allow me to shepherd his life?" Jesus asked. "Yes, yes I am," Gabriel said. "Go up to your spiritual Mount Moriah and lay your Isaac on the altar as a sacrifice, and I will use him greatly for my glory," Jesus said. Without hesitation Gabriel laid one hand on the baby and one hand on Melissa, and he offered the baby up to the Lord. When they got finished praying he told Melissa to name the baby Isaac. Melissa and Gabriel rejoiced the rest of the day for baby Isaac. They knew they were in the will of God naming him that. The nurse came in for the name on the birth certificate. They already picked Isaac out for the first name, but they had no middle name. They decided to name him after the man that God used on Azuza street. Isaac Seymour. To some the name was peculiar and didn't make sense. To Gabriel and Melissa the name was symbolic of what God did this past summer, and how they came to be.

Some people were critical of Gabriel and Melissa. That did not deter them a bit. They held their head high because they knew they were in the plan of God. Gabriel was determined to remain on the potters wheel so he could be a vessel of honor unto the Lord. All the talk and persecution they were to endure was just par for the course. The couple remained stead fast and unmovable throughout their whole sophomore year. Gabriel was named president of the Friends in Christ Club for the next school year. He knew full well what Jeremiah 29:11 was about. God knew the plans he had for Gabriel. Although the road was bumpy at times, Gabriel knew he had to remain steadfast and let God be in control. The best was yet to come.

# CHAPTER 5

That Summer Gabriel and Melissa were on another missionary trip. This time their church group went to the place where the Brownsville Revival was held. Like Azuza the year before, the atmosphere was filled with electricity. Oh how Gabriel wished he was alive when these great moves took place. He decided to go up to the pulpit and sit to pray. As he prayed something amazing happened.

He was translated. He had visions and dreams of going to Heaven and other places, but he was never translated anywhere. When he arrived to where he was translated, there were two figures standing by a beautiful flowing river waiting for him. Both of them were dressed like what Gabriel knew as cavemen. One of the men appeared to be very old, yet he had the vigor of a teenager. The other was much younger and looked almost like the older gentleman. As Gabriel greeted them his mind went through the old and new testament.

They both had on camels skins. They both had wild hair and beards. Both were eating locust and wild honey. This must be Elijah and John. As Gabriel was pondering, John spoke up. "I am John the Baptist Gabriel," John said. "I've come to tell you to never lose sight of your identity. Do you realize, if I knew who I really was I could have done great exploits in my life?," John asked him. "No, John, will you explain yourself?" Gabriel asked John.

"I was the modern day Elijah. Everyone around me, including the Pharisees and Sadducee's saw it, but I never did. One even asked me if I was Elijah, and I told them boldly I was not. The only thing I will be remembered for is baptizing Jesus. Not that it is a bad thing, but if I would have known who I was, I could have done so much more," John said.

"Why didn't you know?" Gabriel asked. "Satan had me blinded to my true identity," John said. That made sense to Gabriel as John 10:10 says; *the thief (Satan) comes but for to steal, kill, and to destroy.* He can even cause you to be blinded to your true identity, all the while stealing the destiny God had planned for your life.

"My destiny was sealed in my mother's womb. I became my own destiny killer when I denied who I was. I may have even gotten offensive of the fact they called me Elijah. Look at me, do I look like Elijah? Now, I can see the resemblances, but back then, I could not because I was blind. Satan wants your destiny too Gabriel. You are more than a student, husband, father, and football hopeful. You are a vessel on the wheel. What you will become all depends on you. You can settle for fame and fortune on the grid iron, or you can stay on the wheel and live out what God wrote about you before the foundation of the world. The choice is yours," John said.

"Carry the mantle proudly," Elijah spoke up. "Look at my life. I confronted and won the contest between our God and the prophets of Baal. One thing caused me to lose the personal victory. Me. I allowed fear of Jezebel killing me to drive me into a cave. After all the miracles God performed though me, I got scared. Because of that fear, I was disqualified from the greater things, and had to pass the mantle on to someone else," Elijah said. "Your identity is not in who you confront Gabriel. Your identity is in the victories you win. When I got mad and hid in the cave, all the exploits I did for the master was negated. I decided because I was afraid, to jump off the potter's wheel and do things my way. You must not do this Gabriel. If you do, all this will be in vain," Elijah said.

"I was more than a voice crying in the wilderness," John said. I was the modern day Elijah. What would have happened if I would have known that?" John added."You have the opportunity to carve your path in the kingdom of God. Will you choose your own path, or stay on the wheel and allow him to make a road for you?" John asked Gabriel.

As Gabriel was pondering this, a bald man walked up and stood beside Elijah. He was wrapped in what looked like a mantle. The mantle was unique. Although it was one mantle, it looked like two. Gabriel remembered from reading the Bible Elisha received a double portion. This must be what he is wrapped in, the double portion.

"He told me I had to see him leave. He told me I had to see him leave, then I would receive the double portion," Elisha said. "I saw him, and I received it," Elisha went on. "Yes Elisha, you dared to believe," Elijah said. "I really wanted you to stay her with me," Elisha said. "Yes, but the victory came after I left. I was holding you back from not only fulfilling your destiny, but for finishing mine," Elijah said. "You and John both had an assignment. One of you finished, and the other fell short. You had to both finish what I couldn't do. Point people to Jesus," Elijah said.

Gabriel stood there in front of the three men thinking about what they were telling him. There were things in life he was really wanting to do. Dreams he wanted to see come to pass. He could choose his own way. That would be easier. He imagined being a big college football star. Getting that call from the Green Bay Packers. That was his dreams. Were they truly God's dreams for his life? If he chose to follow his own path, he would be in the cave. He would be denying his total destiny. What about his family? By following his way, how does that affect him? Suddenly, he spoke up; "As for me and my house, we will serve the Lord."As he said that, he felt something transfer onto him. "He saw it too Elijah. He saw it too," Elisha said. "What are you talking about?" Gabriel asked. "Elisha's mantle was transferred onto you," Elijah said. "You are in the same lineage I am. However, you can also be in another lineage. John was in my lineage, but Jesus was in not only my lineage, but the lineage of King David. That made him more powerful," Elijah said. This confused Gabriel, but knew he would get his questions answered.

Suddenly Jesus appeared with the three men. "Gabriel, you have a mother and a father. They come from different parents and families. Just like me, I share a lineage with Elijah and with David. As my father allows me to mold you, and you give him permission, your lineage is being created. That is how you become a vessel of honor. John told you he lost his way. Elijah told you he was scared and lost out. Your destiny can either fail or be successful on how you handle being molded on the potter's wheel. Father wants me to break you a little and put some pressure on you. It is not to punish you, but to mold you more into our image. Trust the process," Jesus said. "I'm a little worried about the words break you and put the pressure on, but if you will help me, not my will but yours," Gabriel told Jesus. "Gabriel, my grace is sufficient for you," Jesus said.

Soon Gabriel was back in his body praying. He learned some very valuable things talking to Elijah, Elisha, and John. He wanted to make an impact on his world for God. Now he had the keys and secrets to do it. He had the mantle of Elisha and Elijah, but was that all he had?

Soon he finished praying. As he looked around he begin to see what used to be in Brownsville. He saw the success and the failure of this move of God. "Oh God, help me make a difference. Help me usher in a new move of God," Gabriel prayed with tears flowing down his face.

As they left the place where the revival was, Gabriel felt as if he was not alone. He felt he had an extra nudge to help him on his way. He told Melissa what happened, and she told him about her experience with Kathryn Kuhlman. God was doing some amazing things in their family. Some you could see right away, while some of the things were yet to be seen. All Gabriel and Melissa knew to do was wait upon the Lord for their next move. They were ready .

# CHAPTER 6

So much warfare in Gabriel and Melissa's house. It took place right after they got back from the missionary trip. For a couple days things were great. They were pondering on what took place. Suddenly, in the mail, was a letter from a boy that was in Melissa's past. They dated off and on for a few years. He was Melissa's last boyfriend. They lost contact when he moved away. He wrote her to tell her he was moving back into the area and still liked her.

Melissa was happy with Gabriel, and had no intentions of messing that up. She ignored the letter until Gabriel found it. Suddenly, jealousy tried to rise up. He wanted to jump on her case right away. "Resist the devil and he will flee from you," a voice said within him. "I rebuke you Satan in the name of Jesus," Gabriel said. The feeling seemed t ease up, but they didn't totally go away.

When he finally went to see Melissa about the letter, they calmly talked it out. She assured Gabriel she was his forever, and no one was coming between them. Soon they were praying together, and God gave them victory over this.

A couple months went by and again they were faced with a storm. Melissa assured Gabriel there was nothing for him to worry about in their relationship. This was put to the test when another letter was found in Melissa's possession. It was from the same person. He was going to be in town and wanted to see Melissa. This troubled Gabriel greatly. He desperately wanted to trust Melissa, but two letters in a row? Was this a coincidence? He kept the letter to himself, rather choosing to pray about it.

As Gabriel was praying, he and Melissa both were translated to the throne room. The throne room was huge and beautiful just as Gabriel remembered. When they got there they were met by not only Jehovah, but Jesus sitting on his right hand. Jesus was wearing a white robe with a blue sash. On his head was a crown. It was not a crown of thorns, but a royal crown.

As soon as they approached the throne, the scene changed into a large courtroom. Standing in the court room was an eerily dark figure. Gabriel knew within himself it was Satan, but why? Jehovah ordered Satan to step forward and face him. Satan stepped forward carrying a huge book. "What is that you are carrying?" Jehovah asked. "Why, it's the book of deeds. The book of deeds, and I've come to present them to the court," Satan said.

Suddenly Jehovah raised his right hand and the book of deeds fell to the ground. "Denied," Jehovah said. "Denied?" Satan asked. "Yes, denied," Jehovah said. "Do you know who I am?" Satan asked. "I know who you are. I created you," Jehovah said. "I'm the accuser and boy do I have a great accusation against Melissa," Satan snarled.

"What did she do?" Jehovah asked. "Thou shalt not commit adultery," Satan said. "Melissa has been receiving letters from another man while she is married to Gabriel," Satan added. "Do you have any proof of this?" Jehovah asked. "Why yes, in the book of deeds," Satan said. "Where is this book of deeds?" Jehovah asked. "On the floor where you made it fall,"

Jehovah looked past Satan and looked to Jesus. Jesus stood to his feet and stretched out his arms. As he did, blood began to flow out of his hands onto Melissa's head. Melissa stood there like Joshua the high Priest did in the old testament. Suddenly, her garments of sin was changed into a robe of righteousness. "What do you say Jesus?" Jehovah asked. "Redeemed," Jesus said.

Jehovah looked hard at Satan as he began to cower away from the throne. "Get out of here Satan. What the blood cleansed it cannot be dirty again," Jehovah said. "I'll be back," Satan said as he ran out of the courtroom.

Jesus looked at Melissa with eyes of compassion. "Although you did not respond to the letters you are redeemed. He will try something else to break you and Gabriel up, but I am your rear guard, and I will give angels charge over you and you family. Go and sin no more," Jesus said.

Suddenly both Gabriel and Melissa were back in their home holding each other. Gabriel was so thankful he went to the Lord in prayer instead of blaming Melissa for anything. This was proof that with God, they can endure anything thrown their way.

Shortly after Gabriel and Melissa's translation, Jesus appeared to Gabriel. He looked different then he did when they were translated. He had on a white satin robe with a red sash. It appeared he was sitting at a wheel.

Gabriel watched as he quietly began a work no the wheel. As he was working, the clay needed reworked. Gabriel watched as Jesus lovingly and tenderly took the clay in his hands and crushed what he was making. He began to knead the clay and stretch the clay. Soon he put the clay back on the wheel and started the process over again. "He that hath started a good work in you will complete it," Jesus said as he continued working. Gabriel watched as Jesus began spinning the pot. Suddenly, Jesus was standing beside Gabriel with the finished product in his hands.

The finished product was so beautiful. There were no blemishes in it. The pot was smooth and shiny. "If the clay would have said to the potter I don't need you, this pot would not have been made," Jesus said. "Lord, why did Melissa and I take this hit on our marriage?" Gabriel asked. "It was all in the plans," Jesus said. "Plans?" Gabriel asked. "Yes, we had to see what you and her were made of. She never liked this person. She is devoted to you, but we had to remove the hedge of protection from around your marriage to see how you took the pressure. Like the pot, you had to be crushed, and kneaded, and stretched to see if you would be pliable in my hands," Jesus said.

"Why did Satan bring her before the father?" Gabriel asked. "He is not called the accuser of the brethren for no reason. It is his job to accuse, but my blood erases all guilt. Yes, she was wrong in keeping the letters a secret allowing you to find them, but my blood said she was no adulteress," Jesus said

Gabriel began to understand what took place. He never thought of her as a cheater. They have been through too much in their lives to think anything like that. At first, Gabriel was unsure, but when he found the second letter, his spirit told him to go into prayer. It was in listening to his inner man that Melissa was cleared of all Satan's charges, so Gabriel had to clear her as well.

As the summer rolled on, there were more trips. The youth visited Kathryn Kuhlman's residence. They got to see where she grew up. During their trip to Concordia Missouri Melissa conceived another child. This was a happy time for them, The night was just right for the miracle to happen. They had came out of a wonderful service. Gabriel ministered to the youth on forgiveness. There were souls saved and relationships mended.

After the service when Melissa and Gabriel were alone, she surprised him with a pleasant surprise. He did not know she was holding onto special nightwear for a special occasion until now. She came out of the bathroom wearing her special outfit. That is when the miracle took place. They would not know of the miracle until a few weeks later.

A couple months after conception, they found out they were having another girl. They pondered on what to name this bundle of joy. Finally, as if a light bulb went off in their heads, they came up with Miracle Hope. It was an unusual name, but one that was timely. God had performed a miracle in their marriage, and gave them a sense of renewed hope. It was not burdensome to name the child Miracle Hope. When they are asked about the name, they have an opportunity to share how they came up with such name. God could really do wonders in marriages just by using a name.

# CHAPTER 7

For the remainder of their high school days Melissa was home schooled. Miracle Hope developed some medical issues, and Melissa wanted to stay home and take care of her. Gabriel remained active in the Friends in Christ Club. While he enjoyed the club very much, the fact was, he missed Melissa being there by his side at school.

Gabriel began putting himself in Jesus' place when he was in the Garden of Gethsemane. Yes, the disciples were probably a stones throw away from where Jesus was praying, but he still had that lonely feeling. Gabriel wondered if it was the loneliness that caused him to sweat great drops of blood. Melissa was his wife, and the mother of his children, but Gabriel still had that lonely feeling because she was not with him. "I'm a friend that sticks closer than a brother," Jesus whispered into Gabriel's spirit. This seemed to calm Gabriel down a bit.

Miracle began taking a turn for the worse right before Christmas break, Gabriel's senior year. She was diagnosed with acute asthma. Gabriel was in a tight spot. Yet he had an obligation to his family, but he also had the football college scholarship. God would not let him play football throughout his high school years, and he loved playing so much. Gabriel knew he had a tough choice to make. He decided to make the choice on his knees instead of with his head.

As he was praying, he was translated to mountain. He was standing tall on this mountain, and under him was the most scenery he ever saw. To the left of where he was standing was his football career. To the right of where he was standing, although it appeared to be off in the distance was his family. Standing beside Gabriel was Jesus. He did not have that same jovial look he always has when Gabriel sees him. Today, his look was somber. Gabriel could tell he was getting ready to receive a teachable moment. "Look at all this to the right, the left and in front of you. It appears you have everything going for you, doesn't it?" Jesus asked him.

"Yes, Jesus I guess it does," Gabriel replied. "What if suddenly you lost it all? Jesus asked. Gabriel began thinking about his football opportunity, when suddenly, as if Jesus was reading his mind replied; "Is football more important than my best for you?" "No, Lord, you're best is of importance to me," Gabriel replied. "It is true Gabriel you may be good on the grid iron. You may even have professional teams trying to secure you, but without my best in your life, what do you have?", Jesus asked.

Suddenly it was as if the football scene disappeared. Standing off in the distance was the scene of his family. Closer to him was the scene of his family with Jesus in it. Behind him was a scene of his family without Jesus. This scene troubled Gabriel. In this scene, Gabriel was the big football star. His children had grown up, and Melissa had moved on with her life. All Gabriel had was his football career. He appeared to be old and run down looking. "What would you have me do?" Gabriel asked.

"What does it profit a man to gain the whole world and lose the most important commodity in life, his soul. What can you really give in exchange for your soul Gabriel?" Jesus asked. Suddenly

Joshua came and stood beside Jesus. He was dressed as a commander. "Choose ye this day whom you will serve," Joshua said. "Who is your God? Is football your God? Is Jehovah your God? You must choose one. As for me and my house, we will serve the Lord," Joshua added. Suddenly Gabriel was left alone. He had a lot to think about. What was he going to choose? Was the glitz and glamour of football worth losing it all? Was football going to cause a rift in his family? Suddenly, it was as if the answer was staring him in the face the whole time. There is a hungry world out there. They are not hungry for his football prowess, although some like watching him play. They are hungry for what he offers spiritually. Even Peter and john recognized this when they told the lame man at the gate, "Silver and gold have I none, but such as I have, I give to thee." What he has to offer is more important than any football scholarship. He must do what God wants him to do, because Gabriel is the clay, but God is the potter.

A week later the Friends in Christ Club planned an outreach weekend at the high school gymnasium. There is going to be worship music, a Christian band from the First Apostolic church in the town over is going to be providing the worship. Gabriel heard this band when, along with the family, they attended a revival service. There are four singers, which as they sing, the place is charged with an electrifying presence of God that it will make the hairs on your body stand up. They have a drummer that ends up dancing in the middle of the concert. A lead guitarist, bass guitarist, and a keyboard player. You can feel the love of God from not only the singers, but the musicians as well.

Much to his surprise, Gabriel was asked to be the speaker that weekend. He has never spoke in public before. He did not want to say no, as this could be another part of the testing process, and he wanted to pass this test. He agreed to be the speaker. *Now faith is the substance of things hoped for, the evidence of things not seen.* He was going to have to depend on the leading of the Lord to get him through this weekend. Why couldn't they asked his father in law? He is a seasoned pastor. The Lord read Gabriel's thoughts and replied "Yes they could have used your father in law. To the world, that is the logical choice. I wanted to use you. Are you going to be another Jonah?" "No, no I'm not. I'll do it, but you will have to enable me," Gabriel said. "Does not my word say; I can do all things through Christ which strengthens me?" God asked. "Yes it does,"Gabriel replied. "Trust in my strength," God said.

Gabriel turned on some christian music and began to be in deep meditation. Suddenly there came a song on he had never heard before. As he was meditating he heard these words; *Potter mold me, till I'm true. Jesus make me just like you. Anything Lord, to be a vessel for your anointing. Potter break me, even more. Bend me Jesus, till you're sure. You'd be proud to brig this worthless vessel home.* As the song was playing Gabriel had both hands raised high in the air and tears flowing down his cheeks.

He was shown a vision of the potter on the potter's wheel as he had countless times before. In this particular vision, something was different. The potter looked the same, but the clay looked totally different. On that wheel was Gabriel. He watched as the potter took him, and with tender care began to shape him. He could feel those hands shaping him. The hands were sturdy but very loving.

Suddenly, Gabriel began to develop a crack in him. The potter didn't get mad and toss him aside. He gingerly and lovingly picked Gabriel up, and began to reform him. Round and round and round on the wheel Gabriel began to spin. He saw worry begin to leave. Stress begin to leave. Everything Gabriel was struggling with begin to leave as he was being spun on the wheel.

"I know my clay son. I know every strength and I also know every flaw. In front of my wheel is the blueprint of what I want you to look like. There are times when you begin to take on a different form than is on the blueprint. Life begins to happen and you get out of shape and character. I never throw my work away. There is always room for improvement, and I never change the blueprint. I just carefully and lovingly take my project and reshape and reform until they begin to look like the blueprint again. Trust the process and watch what I do," the potter said.

In the midst of the meditation, he developed three sermons to use for that weekend. The one that stuck out the most was Broken Vessel. That sermon fit him so well. He was a broken vessel, but also a work in progress.

He felt impressed to do something he never dreamed he could do. He called the coach and withdrew his scholarship. He told the coach the anointing on his life and his family was more important to him than playing football. The coach tried talking him out of this decision, but Gabriel stood his ground. "I must do what God had called me to do. Football can wait, God can't,"

Gabriel said. "You're a fool Gabriel," the coach said. "You are right coach, I am a fool for Jesus. Football doesn't matter to me anymore. I had fun playing, but I cannot be another Jonah. I just go and do what I know is right," Gabriel said. Melissa stood there listening to the conversation with tears in her eyes. It was true she did not want him to play football anymore, in fact she fasted and prayed he would change his mind. As she listened she quietly thanked God.

For the next several weeks leading up to the event Gabriel began to grow in grace. He was the same husband and father naturally, but he was different on the inside. On the inside of him, he became a giant slayer. There was no problem they faced that he didn't meet with the help of the Lord. Melissa and everyone else associated with Gabriel knew beyond a doubt God has really changed Gabriel. What was in store for Gabriel and Melissa? Only God knew that, but they were both, not just Melissa, willing to wait and see where God took them. It was during this waiting Gabriel heard God ask him a question; "Gabriel, will you carry my word far and wide?" "Yes, I will carry your word far and wide," Gabriel responded. "I want you to finish school at home after this year," God said. "Yes Lord I will do my senior year at home," Gabriel responded.

Gabriel began to grow in intense boldness. The more he prepared for this big event, the more he grew in boldness. "I am going to use you greater than I used Jonah when he finally obeyed me. You will not only see whole cities saved, but states as well. Never neglect the call on your life. It is for this calling you were placed on this earth," God said.

# CHAPTER 8

The weekend of the event finally arrived. This event was showered with much prayer and fasting. The Friends in Christ Club met every morning around the flagpole to pray. The Friday before the event one of the students said the Lord told him to march around the school like they did in Joshua's day. God was not only going to give them the school, but the region. Another member, a shy girl that hardly says anything in school or the club meetings chimed in. She told how the Lord gave her a dream about the club walking around the town the day of the event praying for not only the town, but the surrounding region. Suddenly, Gabriel got a confirmation in his spirit. He told the club leader both things needed to be done.

Soon the club was marching around the school seven times praying like the children of Israel marched around in Joshua's day. As the marched, you could feel the charge of the Holy Ghost sweeping over the school grounds. They decided to march inside the school as well. Soon, they were standing at the doorway of the Health class praying god would work a work.

The health department decided the year before to take a stand against teen pregnancy. They put condom machines in all the boy's bathrooms. The morning after pill was placed in each of the girl's bathrooms. Not long after they were installed, you would see students sneak into secluded places and have sex. Many students were expelled because of the incidents. The club has been praying God would shut the program down. As they prayed, you could feel something was fixing to take place. Sure enough, an hour after they prayed for God to work a work, the machines began to come down. Hall monitors were put in place, especially in those secluded paces. Students were no longer allowed to kiss or hold hands while on school property. Revival was certainly in the air.

The next morning they marched around the town. As they marched, you could feel a surge of power going throughout the whole area. Parents were making up with their children over fights they were having. Husband and wives were reuniting in the home. Bars were starting to close down. Many other notable events began happening that day as revival was in the air.

That night the gymnasium was powerfully charged. People were flocking in to try and get front row seats. Chairs were placed all around the gym floor as the crowds began pouring in. Suddenly, the moment had arrived. At 7 o'clock the pastor of the Apostolic church made his way center stage. The musicians and singers were already there in a circle praying and seeking God. As the service started the performers took their spots. The pastor prayed then let the group take over.

The drummer began doing a drum roll to get the crowd moving. As he hit the cymbals in unison, the singers slowly began to sing How Great Thou Art. By now, the crowd was on their feet, with hands lifted in the air singing and worshiping. You could feel the electricity in the air. Something was fixing to take place. High worship lasted an hour, when suddenly, Gabriel was turned loose.

Melissa could not tell he was nervous. He took the microphone in his hand, and became a different person. He began calling people out of their seat and prophesying over them. Was this her Gabriel? The shy and timid Gabriel that was once the clay, that now seemed to be the finished product? Was this the same Gabriel that sat in the front of the now empty church where the Azuza Street revival took place and got the mantle of William Seymour? Was this the same Gabriel that God took to Heaven and allowed him to talk to various heroes of the faith? It looked like the same Gabriel, yet he was more refined. More anointed than she ever saw before.

As she looked at him, she noticed standing on the right and left of him were ministering angels. As he walked, they walked. As he lifted his hands, they lifted their hands. She was totally amazed at how far this kid, the football guru had come. As he ministered to the people he called up they began to get healed, delivered and set free. Was he going to be able to deliver the message he prepared?

Suddenly he walked to the podium and began to speak. He preached in Jeremiah where the potter made again another vessel. He began to share all the things that were taking place in his life. As he shared, people began running to the altar again. Salvation was coming to the lost. The Holy Ghost was being poured out on the hungry. The first night of the revival was certainly power packed to say the least.

Each night something different took place. By the time the weekend was concluded, 95 souls were saved. 15 received the Holy Ghost, and 29 were healed and delivered. God moved in ways if it were not recorded Gabriel would not have believed. The results the region experienced was amazing as well. The region was declared a dry region. All the bars were permanently closed. Abortion clinics were closed. Strip clubs were closed. Prostitutes were taken off the streets. Many more notable things began to take place as one obedient person was willing to leave his dream and devote himself to the hands of the potter.

Gabriel began taking his message to other regions. He held six revivals in the weeks that followed. He even held a revival on Azuza Street. God re birthed the Azuza Street revival. This time, William Seymour wasn't the evangelist. Gabriel was the one doing the preaching. Gabriel and Melissa ended up having one more child. They named her Joy because after all they endured, serving the Lord gave them the most joy. Only God knows the magnitude of what Gabriel has become. Seems like when the clay becomes the clay, and allows the potter to become the potter, the potter shows up and shows out. Gabriel truly was a broken vessel.

# EPILOGUE

The day I sat and watched the potter at work really changed my life. It was mind blowing watching him at work. I noticed it took patience to do what he was doing. He could have stopped working at the first sign of a flaw, but he didn't. He, like God, took that clay and reworked it.

The words Jeremiah spoke while he was in a vision at the potter's house was a foundational stone for this story. He made it again another vessel. You may have bought this book , whether the digital of hard copy, downloaded it or opened it up, and was broken inside when you read the first word. Remember, he made it again another vessel. As I sit here at this keyboard, the song the Original Hinsons wrote and recorded is again going over inside me. Potter mold me till I'm true. Jesus make me just like you. Anything Lord to be a vessel for your anointing. Potter break me even more. Bend me Jesus till you're sure. You'd be proud to bring this worthless vessel home.

Whether you realize it or not everyone is broken. Gabriel was broken several times. Another song says the potter knows the clay. How much p[pressure it can take. How many times around the wheel. Till it sufficient to his will. He's planned a beautiful design. Yet will take some fire and time. You're going to be okay. The potter knows the clay. Whether yo think you have it all together or not, at some point you were broken. I was broken. But know this, the potter knows the clay.

# Don't miss out!

Visit the website below and you can sign up to receive emails whenever Tracy Henderson publishes a new book. There's no charge and no obligation.

https://books2read.com/r/B-A-XBQU-EUKSC

**BOOKS 2 READ**

Connecting independent readers to independent writers.

# Also by Tracy Henderson

**Family Mantle**
Gabbi's Amazing Dream
Gabbi's Heavenly Visitation
The Judge and the Prophet

**Inheritance Series**
Finish Strong. A Story About Spiritual Inheritance
Power With God

**Standalone**
'When I See the Blood
The Visitation That Changed the Town
Our Coat. His Purpose
To Love Again
Broken Vessel

# About the Author

Writing has been a passion of mine since I was in school. I was top writer in my Creative Writing class in 8th grade. I write from the heart and not the head. When you read my material, you are not only reading a book, but are looking in the window of my soul.

# **About the Publisher**

Contact US at:

Greater Deliverance Ministries
16584 N IL Hwy 37 Lot 66
Mount Vernon, Illinois. 62864
proudauthor67@outlook.com
(618)315-5479
Cashapp: $proudauthor67

www.ingramcontent.com/pod-product-compliance
Lightning Source LLC
Chambersburg PA
CBHW021347160726
47994CB00007B/2863